The Quilt-Maker's Scrap

AMY L. LAURENS

OTHER WORKS

SANCTUARY SERIES

Where Shadows Rise
Through Roads Between
When Worlds Collide

KADITEOS SERIES

How Not To Acquire A Castle
How Not To Ring The Hero's Bell
How Not To Take Over The World

SHORT STORY COLLECTIONS

Of Sea Foam and Blood
Darkness and Good

NON-FICTION

How To Write Dogs
How To Theme
How To Create Cultures

Find other works by the author at
www.amylaurens.com

The Quilt-Maker's Scrap

INKLET #24

AMY L. LAURENS

Inkprint PRESS

www.inkprintpress.com

Print ISBN: 978-1-925825-22-0
eBook ISBN: 9781386354932

www.inkprintpress.com

National Library of Australia Cataloguing-in-Publication Data
Laurens, Amy 1985 –
The Quilt-Maker's Scrap
26 p.
ISBN: 978-1-925825-22-0
Inkprint Press, Canberra, Australia
1. Fiction—Christian—Classic & Allegory 2. Fiction—Short Stories

First Print Edition: December 2019
Cover design © Inkprint Press
Interior art © Amy Laurens

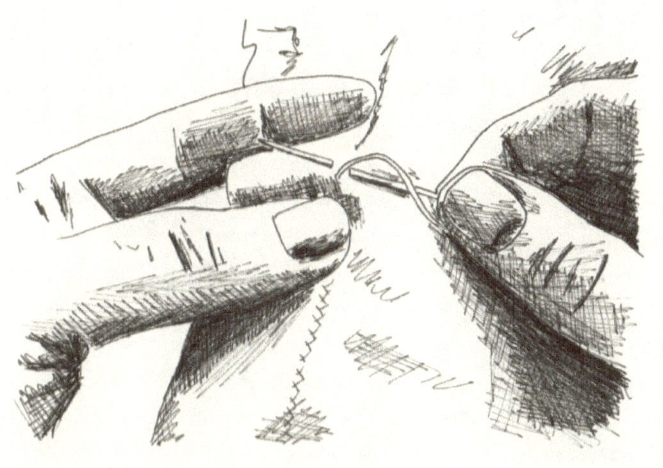

THE QUILT-MAKER'S SCRAP

Once, in a Quilt-maker's basket, there lived a scrap of fabric. All the other scraps in the basket had something special about them: some were smooth and soft, others were warm and furry, and still others had bright colors or pretty patterns. But this scrap was dull and ugly and rough.

The other scraps teased him. "The Quilt-maker will never choose you," said a scrap of silver satin. "Not when she could choose me. Look how I glimmer in the light!"

"Or me!" said a golden scrap who had shining sequins sewn onto her. "I could dazzle anyone!"

"Any quilt with *you* in it," said a scrap of sensible navy wool, "would be an embarrassment."

The little scrap drooped. The other scraps were right—he was dull and ugly and boring. No one would want him in a quilt. A piece of cream poplin brushed past him. "You never know," she said. "Maybe the Quilt-maker will make a quilt for someone she doesn't like. Then it wouldn't matter if it was ugly."

Even though she had meant to be mean, the poplin's words gave the little dull scrap hope. Maybe the Quilt-maker *would* make an ugly quilt. He wouldn't mind, not at all. At least then he'd have a home—and no one would tease him anymore. So he waited near the top of the basket, hoping that someday the Quilt-maker would choose him.

Months passed, and many new scraps came and went.

The beautiful scraps, the ones that were silky or shiny, warm or soft, didn't stay for very long, some spending less than a day in the basket before the Quilt-maker took them out again. The little dull scrap began to grow tired of the other scraps' taunts, but still he stayed near the top of the basket, waiting and hoping.

One day, just before Christmas, the Quilt-maker's hand reached into the basket. She sifted through the scraps, looking for the right one to use. She picked up a scarlet scrap of silk.

"Ah ha!" he called to his friends. "She likes my colour. She'll choose me, no doubt!" But as he spoke, the hand lowered him back into the basket.

Next she chose a warm, soft piece of fleece. "She likes my warmth!" he called. "She'll use me for sure."

But he too returned to the basket.

At last the Quilt-maker came to the little dull scrap. She lifted him gently out of the basket and peered at him through her glasses.

"Yes," she whispered. "This is just what I need."

The little dull scrap could hardly believe it. How could Quilt-maker need *him?*

Soon the Quilt-maker finished the quilt. Everyone who saw it exclaimed over its beauty, and the Quilt-maker entered it into a quilt show. The little scrap knew that *he* didn't make the quilt beautiful, but the idea of going to a show excited him so much that it didn't matter.

The day for the show arrived, and all the entrants hung up their quilts. The Quilt-maker hung her quilt opposite a large window and placed her nametag on the wall next to it before wandering off to have a look at the other entries.

The little scrap of fabric sat contentedly, watching the people pass by. Many of them stopped to admire his quilt. Some even stepped forward to examine it closely. He'd never seen so many people before, and it was all very exciting.

At last it was time for the judging. The sun sank towards the horizon and the crowds thinned, giving the little dull scrap some time to think. He couldn't believe how many people had come to see the quilt that he was so fortunate to be a part of. He'd even had a sneaking suspicion that a few times, some of the people had been looking at *him*.

But he must have imagined it, considering how ugly and insignificant he was. And after all, he was just one piece in the whole quilt.

The judges arrived, and inspected every inch of the quilt with great care. They stopped to admire the lovely colours of the fabric that the Quilt-maker had used for a woman's dress. They exclaimed over the brightness of the star at the top of the quilt. They wondered at the detail in the people's faces.

Finally, they turned to the middle of the quilt where the little dull scrap waited nervously. A gentle finger reached out to touch him, moving over his rough, unfinished surface.

"It's perfect," they whispered to each other.

The little scrap stared in disbelief.

The judges drew away to confer with one another, heads bowed, whispering. Then they straightened, and addressed the room. "This is the final quilt," they said, "and it is by far the best. We declare this quilt the winner."

A cheer went up from the crowd and they parted to let the Quilt-maker through.

As they did, the little scrap looked up at the window. Night had fallen, turning the glass into a mirror.

He hadn't seen the quilt before, and he stared. There he sat, right in the very centre of the quilt. A golden glow streamed out from all around him, and people knelt and presented gifts of gold, incense and myrrh. But that wasn't the best part. Just above him lay a small scrap of purest white, sewn in the shape of a baby. And as he sat watching the reflection while the crowd celebrated below, he realised what he had become.

He was the manger, and even though in the basket he'd been ugly and boring and rough, the Quilt-maker believed he was special enough to hold the newborn Saviour.

THE MAKING OF
THE QUILT-MAKER'S SCRAP

I'm pretty sure this was one of those stories that my mum actually thought up, and asked me to write for her. I vaguely recall another one, something about the king's bananas. She's pretty good at parable-style stories, to be honest, and I'm super glad I've finally convinced her to publish a picture book (life goal: affiliate EVERYONE with the book industry!).

So: thank you, Mum, for the story idea! I'm glad it turned out alright ☺

DOWNLOAD YOUR FREE EBOOK

When you buy a print book from Inkprint Press, we like to say THANK YOU by offering you the ebook for free!

Please head to
www.inkprintpress.com/inklets/24/
and the use the coupon INK24LET to get your copy of this Inklet in epub AND mobi today!
(Coupon will only work once.)

Read more by this author!

WHERE YOUR TREASURE IS

In a series of plays written for a teen audience, *Where Your Treasure Is* explores a variety of Christian concepts, from the real meaning of trust, freedom and forgiveness, to the importance of exercising the gifts we have been given. Plays range from 8 to 70 minutes and usually require 6 or 8 actors.

DRIVE:

Two apparently unrelated teens learn what it means to both trust and be trusted. (70 mins, 8 actors)

WHERE YOUR TREASURE IS:
Pirates set off in search of the King's treasure and discover the real meaning of forgiveness. (40 mins, 6 actors)

THE 5000:
Three different perspectives on the feeding of the five thousand. (8 mins, 6 actors)

GIFTS:
A group of teens compare the gifts they received for Christmas—physical and spiritual. (10 mins, 6 actors)

TURNING POINT:
The story of King Manasseh demonstrates the importance of repentance. (30 mins, 8 actors)

IN SEARCH OF FREEDOM:
A group of teens left behind after the Exodus discover the real meaning of freedom. (25 mins, 8 actors)*

THE JOURNEY:
The Israelites' journey across the desert to the Promised Land is hard, but God is always there. (20 mins, 9 actors) (An unconnected sequel to IN SEARCH OF FREEDOM.)

* Warning: While none of the plays are astoundingly correct for the time period they're set in (except perhaps *Turning Point*), *In Search of Freedom* in particular is almost entirely composed of anachronistic speech and concepts. Fair warning. It doesn't really take itself seriously!

Reading them now! Head to http://www.amylaurens.com/books/plays-poetry/where-your-treasure-is/ to buy your copy now!

ABOUT THE AUTHOR

AMY L. LAURENS is one of the pennames of Amy Laurens—the 'L' in the middle denotes a specifically Christian book. Amy's written a couple of those, but more often she writes secular fantasy novels. She has written a middle grade portal fantasy trilogy (the *Sanctuary* series) set in Nowra, Australia, and the Kaditeos series of humorous fantasy stories, starting with *How Not To Acquire A Castle*.

You can find out more about Amy at her website, www.amylaurens.com.

INKLETS

Collect them all! Released on the 1st and 15th of each month.

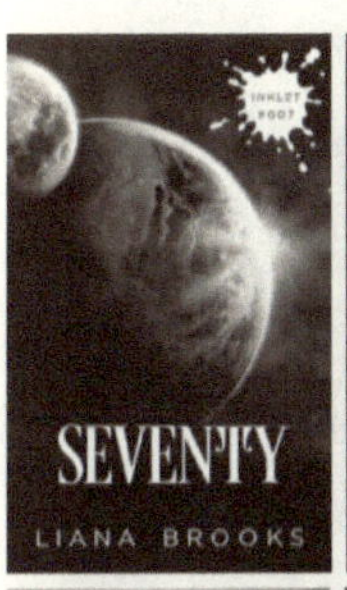
SEVENTY
LIANA BROOKS

A Final Request
for Mercy
AMY LAURENS

the kitten psychologist
vs.
the kitten's owners
THEA VAN DIEPEN

Answer the
Question
AMY LAURENS

Happily,
Red
AMY LAURENS

the kitten psychologist
tries to be patient
through email
THEA VAN DIEPEN

DRAGON
TUESDAY
AMY LAURENS

RED PLANET
REFUGEES
LIANA BROOKS

the kitten psychologist &
What The Kitten Did
THEA VAN DIEPEN

INKLET #016
Cherry Blossom
AMY LAURENS

Alone
AMY LAURENS

INKLET #018
the kitten psychologist
& The Kitten
Come To A Conclusion
THEA VAN DIEPEN

LEVEL NINE
LIANA BROOKS

INKLET #020
To Dust
AMY LAURENS

INKLET #021
Interchange
AMY LAURENS

INKLET #022
Emalia's Lanterns
LIANA BROOKS

INKLET #023
Dear Santa
AMY LAURENS

INKLET #024
The Quilt-Maker's Scrap
AMY L LAURENS